Views from the Balcony

This is a work of fiction. All the characters and events portrayed in this novel are either fictitious or are used fictitiously.

VIEWS FROM THE BALCONY
Copyright © 2015 by Kevin Shoemaker

This book is printed on acid free paper

A Shoemaker Labs Book
Indian Harbour Beach, Florida

e-mail: Shoemakerlabs@gmail.com

All Rights Reserved

ISBN 978-0-9815092-0-4
ISBN 0-9815092-0-4

Registered with the Library of Congress

Grateful acknowledgement is made to those who have given permission for the use of previously copyrighted material in this book. Every reasonable care has been taken to correctly acknowledge copyright ownership. The author and publisher would welcome information that will enable them to rectify any errors or omissions in succeeding printings.

Cover Art courtesy of Integrative Ink

First edition March, 2015
Printed in the United States of America

Dedicated to Bruce Morosohk
A good loving person
A wonderful husband and father
We will all miss you

Acknowledgment

I would like to sincerely like to thank Jack Shoemaker for his editing and comments. Also, I would like to thank my friends Ed, Joy and Savannah for their editing and comments. Finally, I would like to thank my daughter Leah and son Stephen, for their encouragement and patience.

Introduction

This book comprises a set of pictures taken from my balcony in Indian Harbour Beach, Florida along with a story woven through it. Over a period of 12 months starting in the summer of 2012, the author set up a tripod with a Nikon D5100 camera using 50 and 300 mm lenses to take the pictures herein. The balcony is situated on the Atlantic Ocean approximately 20 miles south of Cape Canaveral and the Kennedy Space Center. During this period of time, one of the retired Space Shuttles was transferred from the Cape to Washington, D.C., and flew directly over us. It left the Cape, flew south along the coast to Melbourne as a tribute to all of the space workers who had worked on the fleet for so long. Many thousands of space workers had been laid off by this time and ironically were not present to see the fly by. My neighbor, C. Wayne Blanchard actually took the best photo of the event which is in this book and is credited here. Judi Morosohk is also credited with photos on pages 13 and 14.

Life on the ocean can be wondrous, as proven here by these images. We are but inches away from a completely different environment which changes daily. Although humans have adapted to the ocean, they will never master it. The dynamics of the water, atmosphere and shore line defy control. They also remind us not only of their unpredictable temper, welcoming beauty and changing mood but also of their role in the cycle of life. The pre-Socratic philosophers Thales, Heraclitus and Parmenides argued about the role of water in the overall scheme of existence. Thales was convinced that all things came from water, Heraclitus and Parmenides discussed whether or not water was always changing or always the same. From the balcony, it is all of these things.

This is a picture book in a sense and represents 24 hours of images. Of course the story took a lot longer than a day, but not much longer.

I live within view of the rocket launches from Cape Canaveral, which always take place in good weather. My first launch experience was late at night, in very clear dark skies. By the time the last flickers of rocket plume were fading into the constellation Orion, the rocket was nearing Africa.

The sight was extraordinary and was the impetus for purchasing a decent camera. The launches happen about once a month and any time of day based solely on a mathematically derived time "window" to optimize trajectory and minimize fuel burn.

These events happen when looking to the left while on the balcony. Looking straight out allows one to witness cruise ships, large fish leaping out of the water, sun rises, moon rises, fishing vessels and the best lightning displays during stormy weather. Looking to the right of center is in the direction of the Bahamas where the cruise ships in this area typically head for. Also, when looking down at the sandy beach, the life encrusted coral reefs are exposed during low tide. This tidal cycle not only exposes the reefs but also brings the wildlife looking for isolated pools of seawater from which to pluck fish.

The birds include heron, seagulls, "skimmers," sand pipers, pelicans and a wide variety of migratory fowl. The cool thing is that for the most part they coexist with the people on the beach and give off the impression that they are just interested in surviving even amongst the giants and curious. This is a good skill for wildlife these days. Large herons will land near some of the many fishermen on the beach and have learned to look for the bait bucket. They quietly close in with their stork like walk towards the fishing poles and tackle boxes then wait. They are experts in looking in the right areas for a snack. They read the fisherman's body language and once a lapse in concentration is detected, they get their prize.

Another amazing discovery just below the balcony is the amount and size of nesting turtles that start coming ashore every May. For the next six weeks they come out of the sea, usually in the very early hours of the morning and lay a clutch of eggs. These turtles, loggerhead and leatherback for the most part, are all endangered. They too are only interested in surviving and do their best to cover their nest, sometimes even create a decoy nest, and get back into the sea before sunrise. One evening the author was awake and on the balcony at around midnight when he observed a large dark mass coming out of the breakers. A large six foot long leatherback came out of the water to lay some eggs. I went down to get a closer look. The animal, whose head was about the same size as mine, looked up, acknowledged my presence, and slowly made her way to the top of the beach where she dug a two foot hole and laid her clutch. The physical effort required to make the fifty foot trek was enormous. She took two or three "steps" with her flippers and then rested. This continued all the way up and back. Once she returned to the water and made it to two foot deep water, the buoyancy effect took over and she was able to glide away almost effortlessly.

On another occasion a turtle was observed coming out of the water early in the evening around 9 pm during the Fourth of July fireworks celebrations on the beach. The crowded area parted as the turtle, this time a loggerhead, came out, made her way through the revelers and laid a clutch of eggs. This is another example of "when its time its time."

Yet another view these days is of boiling water just off shore. This is actually thousands of small fish schooling and leaping out the water, especially when a wave crests. The water explodes with leaping fish, alerting the predatory birds like the pelicans and large fish like tarpon that dinner awaits. The author has observed quite a few porpoise, marlin and "bait" fish over the time he has been on the balcony as well. On many evenings, fishing boats can be seen trolling up and down the cost with large nets gathering the catch prevalent on the submerged reefs.

Historically, the views to the left include not only Kennedy Space Center but also the battlegrounds from several wars. Just to the right of the launch towers and out perhaps ten miles from shore, there lies a U boat amongst several of it's victims in eighty feet of water. Viewing due East covers the area littered with sailing vessels going back to the 1500s that met their fate in battles or hurricanes. Looking further to the right and more Southerly grants you a view of the graveyard of the five ships owned by the Spanish Queen that sank in 1715. A fortune of over a billion dollars in gold is buried there as a result of their demise. That is why that coast is known as the "Treasure" coast. This coast, our coast, where the balcony is situated is aptly named the "Space Coast." Not only are there numerous wrecks of ships off shore but there are also numerous piles of debris from failed rocket launches including, tragically, the Space Shuttle Challenger. From the 1950s on launches were attempted from the Cape to the left of the balcony. During the early parts of this period there were certainly more failures than triumphs and as a result, the ocean floor is littered with aluminum shards, boosters and payloads. Today they are sending more strap on boosters to the depths than failed rockets. The aerospace community has a saying..."Space is hard, but not impossible."

Now on with the story. The views in this book are a compilation of a few months of effort and are organized into the portions of the day. All were taken with a Nikon D5100 SLR camera, mostly on a tripod. Typically I used a remote shutter control to take the picture, this helped minimize vibration. Very few have been post processed and if so, typically to crop the real subject from the rest of the scene. Some have been manipulated using LightBox software to bring out highlights. The amazing thing about cameras like this is that see colors at night, unlike their owners. As a result, several of this images look like daytime shots, with green vegetation and deep blue skies. But in reality they have been taken late at night in sometime very dark conditions. Someone once told me that this kind of photography is like a treasure hunt, where you find unexpected gifts in the image. Good examples of this are the photos of lightning from nearby storms. The faint tendrils and return strikes are visible to the camera and most times not the eye.

Lastly, there is a story that goes with this book, about an engineer who experiences a day like the one portrayed and puts the images into context with her work.

Please enjoy the book as much as I enjoyed writing it and if you have any comments or questions, I can be reached at shoemakerlabs@gmail.com

Thank you,

Kevin O. Shoemaker

A typical morning on the Space Coast
The Sun is about to rise from the East
There is silence with the exception of the faint lapping of the waves
The air is fresh and cool
Standing on the sand in bare feet

A few light taps upon the window pane made Angela Bencomo start her day askew, she looked at the clock, saw 5:30 am and found it nearly impossible to go back to sleep after that. A light rain had started to dampen the balcony and splash against the sliding glass door. At some point after she tried to keep her eyes closed and her mind off of work, she gave up and got out of bed. Like every other morning, the first thing she did was look through the glass door at the sea. Most people who live by the ocean do this, attracted to the beauty and wonder of the scene. Every day is different here, the mood of the water changes frequently, the ocean's inhabitants come and go. The color and temperament change as well, no wonder we are drawn to the display.

She opened the glass door and smelled the sea air. The morning was starting and the clearness of the cool made her think about work and life. The hues and contrasts were starting to bring the colors out of the shades of gray night. She thought about her cup of tea next, turned and walked towards the kitchen to start the process.

A few steps inside did not attenuate the sounds of the surf. It followed her to the sink, where she selected her favorite cup, filled it with water and started to heat it in the microwave oven.

She returned to the balcony to view the colors of the dawn and to await the presentation of the sun. Today she would not be disappointed as blues and whites transitioned to orange and gold. The sun started its ascent into the sky and for a moment it seemed, into the clouds.

Returning to the kitchen, she prepared breakfast and sat down at the glass table with a view out the living room glass door and windows. The sun filled the room and made her squint. Doing this made her feel the slight lack of sleep from the night before. The feeling would dissipate by mid morning but the sensation was always a bit annoying. The lack of sleep came from the demands of her job as a satellite engineer. Recently she had finished a very important project on a mission that she felt was very exciting and certainly something to be proud of. Knowing that a year from the start the experience would bring a sense of gratification, she contributed a piece of her soul by working long hours and pushing her mind to its limits. The effort was worth it but the aftermath was a sense of exhaustion. The effort was not complete however as the satellite she worked on was about to launch and luckily would be seen from her balcony. But that would be much later in the evening.

Today (a Saturday) would be filled with relaxation and a welcome plethora of hours doing very little. She decided earlier in the week that this day would be spent reading, relaxing and sitting on the balcony. She also decided to document the experience with a camera as it unfolded.

After a magnificent sunrise, the colors of the day stabilized into the more normal blues and whites, welcoming the animals and people to the beach. By now the sea had established it's first color of the day. This would be a blue, a good choice of the many it had available. Unbeknownst to most people the sea has a thousand colors and as many moods. The colors are created by the weather, the undercurrents, the position of the sun, the time of day and certainly the time of year. Under the surface sea grass, plankton, sea weed and other occupants move about near the surface and influence the color. The weather of course with different cloud patterns and coverage influence the tint, contrast and hue. But there is yet another influence. One a bit more emotional; the

sea has moods. Angela had seen it angry, for instance during a storm, and content after it's passing. She has also seen it exhausted and melancholy. This of course is a matter of interpretation, but it seems that when the environment is upset or happy, so are its inhabitants and thus this bit of resonance is witnessed from the balcony every hour of every day.

Here at the beach, the inhabitants or visitors seem happy. Many come for vacation and are insisting on being in a good mood. Many who live here find comfort in the view and are thus content. There is a potentially plausible reason for this mood in the chemicals carried off from the mist of the crashing waves, or the ions perhaps that allow us to shed stress and concern. Maybe this is why there are so many parties and weddings on the ocean's edge or maybe this is just an acknowledgement of the fact that those who love life know that it was created here. That the shoreline is the line of demarcation attacked by the organisms whose lungs had developed enough for them to emerge onto the dry land, one step closer to the stars.

Outward Angela looked towards the horizon and at a cloud hosting a rain shower. She thought of the interesting fact that the rain was pure water, refilling the salty sea after having evaporated over some other ocean, lake or river. A profound cycle; one wonders how the organisms feels at the surface of the ocean during these showers and storms. They say that 70% of the Earth is covered by water, when they say this, they usually forget to mention that the atmosphere and the living organisms on the land are mostly water also.

The rest of the universe, starting from our moon has pockets and oceans and vast expanses of water in the form of clouds. Radio astronomers in the 1960s "dialed" in the resonant frequency of water (of which there are a few by the way) and were able to map vast clouds of the substance in space. Since then, the moon, the planet Mars, other moons and comets all have been found with water on them. There is a current theory that the water on Earth and these other environs came to us from millions of comets. How poetic to think that water coalesced in outer space into very large hunks of ice, and having a gravitation pull towards our sun, started to enter into orbits, some very elliptical, many of whom found their way to our planet and populated the surface with trillions of gallons of the fluid.

Here, on Earth, water can exist in all three states, a gas, a solid and a liquid. Is this the requirement for prolific life to occur?

She sat at the table near the window sipping tea, eating her breakfast and observing the beach. It was low tide and many reefs covered with sea grass had emerged. This drew the attention of the local sea birds who came over to the reefs to look for fish caught in isolated pools of water. These birds for the most part are not afraid of humans and many times come quite close, hoping to find food. In reality, they just want to survive, and if that requires living with humans, so be it.

Thinking about her position in life as an engineer and designer of space hardware, she knew it was part of something important but it had not been given to her. She worked hard in college, worked hard during her career and took her tasks very seriously. As a result, others recommended her for increasingly higher positions. Soon she would witness the fruits of her labor from this very balcony.

In actuality, it was a pretty straight forward life. Her dad told her early on to "just do the work." This was his philosophy as he went through school. He did what he was asked and as a result obtained good grades, good opportunities and progressed through college to obtain advanced degrees and eventually teach college for 40 years. "There are lots of smarter people in this world," he would say, "but because some of them get distracted and put off their tasks, they progress at a slower pace and never see the world open up to them." She took this advice to heart and in actuality it was not that hard to take the advice of her teachers and enjoy the fruits of her efforts.

One day she looked up from her desk and realized that she was part of something very important. She would eventually design components for a satellite that would be sent up into orbit, then out into space to become a discovery machine.

Scientists were depending on her equipment to work flawlessly for many years as they reaped the abundance of new details about our universe. Tonight she would see the machinery she designed rocket into the cosmos.

She looked out of the window as she thought about these things and her position in life, which was on the ocean, within a few miles of the launch pad. Although tired from her efforts, tonight would pay her back in appreciation.

Was there magic in her job? Not really. In fact, she ran a computer program at work, much like so many of us do. This program predicted the performance of the equipment she was asked to design for this satellite. Using common sense and a little bit of research, she put in her design for evaluation and had the software dissect the details with mathematics and display the results.

Once the computer completed its task, the results were displayed for her consideration. This was actually the first of many steps. She pondered the design, thought is was reasonable and put together a presentation to show her peers for comment. They would examine her work and "critique as necessary."

Although this step sounds like asking for criticism, it actually gained her the acceptance of a team and thus produced a united front to proceed to the preliminary design review (PDR). So she paid particular attention to her presentation and made it easy to understand by placing conclusions on most pages and then combined them into a summary. It had a good flow to it she thought and before she sent it to the team, she had her immediate boss review it.

"Looks good Angela," was his immediate reaction. He continued, "but remember that you are a specialist in this field and many of the people this will go to are in other disciplines including management. Try to see through their eyes. In other words, what would they be interested in?"

She knew they would be interested in schedule and cost. All tasks are measured in these quantities. Initially, engineers are asked how much and how long particular engineering details will require.

For instance, how long would it take to make a flashlight? The first step is to break down the components and consider each separately. How much is the bulb? How long will it take to get? Fundamental questions that lead to a sophisticated device. How about a satellite? How much is the antenna, how long will it take to design? Once these questions are answered the next step is to consider the amount of risk involved, then the amount of testing required to verify its performance. Again all simple steps leading to a sophisticated device. But for now she took more pictures from the balcony. This was more relaxing and she deserved it after a significant amount of work to complete all of her tasks that led up to the launch tonight.

Then the phone rang. She located the device and answered.

"Hello?"

"Hello Angela, this is Norm."

"Hey Norm. What's up?"

"Well a little problem has come on the payload, can you come to the Cape and help us out?"

"Of course! How bad of a problem?"

"Apparently, one that only you can solve. The antenna control software you wrote is sending us error messages. We think we know what to do but the Vice President of the company wants you to okay the process."

"I'll be right there, Norm. It will take about 20 minutes."

She went into the living room to pick up her backpack and laptop computer. For a moment she peered out of the sliding glass doors.

She saw the ocean boiling, a sign of bait fish. She also saw several very large fish jumping out of the water near the boiling activity. They were feeding and the bait fish were trying to protect themselves by clustering in a tight ball. Safety in numbers is their credo. Angela grabbed the camera and took a quick shot.

"So much action in the sea today," she thought. She put the camera down and looked to the North where the rocket, with her payload, were waiting.

"Problems?" She said out loud. "This antenna has never had any problems."

She grabbed her things and headed out the door. She drove North to the Cape and after showing her badge to the guards at the gate, was allowed into the secured area.

"They're waiting for you," one of them said.

She quickly drove into the fire control compound, parked and ran into the building. Doors were opened for her as she made her way to launch control. As she entered the room it was obvious where the action was. There was a cluster of people around several computer screens.

One of them looked up and said:

"Okay, let me see what's going on."

Several people moved aside and let her work with the primary display. She sat down and looked at the screen for a long moment.

"Who loaded this code?"

"Someone in I&T, Integration and Test."

"Yeah, know what I&T means. The antenna is mad because the code was loaded improperly. Had you launched it like this it never would have worked. This is test code, not operating code. I can fix the problem though....there. Try it now."

The launch technicians restarted their communication test routines and quickly determined that all was well.

"We're good to go, resume the countdown," sounded the launch director while taking his seat. The rest of the controllers returned to their seats and continued the launch activities.

Angela was left alone to monitor the antenna but she knew all was well. A simple mistake had been made.

"You need me anymore?"

"Nope, we're good."

Having seen quite a few launches from inside, she decided to go back to the comfort of her condo to see the event. She again grabbed her things and headed for the door.

"Thanks," she heard from somewhere in the room.

"No problem," was her reply.

She got back in her car and headed home. The launch was still hours away so she had time for lunch and a bit more relaxation on the balcony.

The tide had receded to expose the coral reefs by the time she got home. All was well as the Cape and the idea of her place in the Universe was starting to hit home just as she peered over the railing to view the Ocean. The camera was found and set back on the tripod. A few practice shots were taken (which are in this book). Its hard to anticipate the best settings for an event that is hours away, but sometimes you can get close.

She found a tall chair to sit in and wait for the noise.

As she sat there, her eyes wandered over the beach and she discovered the tracks of a large turtle, who had, late in the evening before, crawled out of the sea to deposit a clutch of eggs. Starting around June and lasting until the end of July, the turtles come out typically around 3-4 AM and dig a hole well away from the surf. Sometimes they dig a hole, lay the eggs, smooth it over gently, then disturb a local area as a decoy. Then they leave the nest using a different path.   Six weeks later the babies emerge and seemingly follow the sound to the surf. Predators are of course around and the survival rate is very low as a result. The babies are attracted to light which necessitates the dousing of street lights and house lights during this period. Once, Angela was out on the beach when a few turtles emerged from the surf. They were huge, one was four foot and the second at least five foot long. The first was a loggerhead and the second a leatherback. Both majestic and determined, they took a few strokes upon the beach, rested, then took a few more in an ancient ritual millions of years old.

Soon they were laying a clutch of eggs, carefully digging a hole, depositing a dozen or so eggs and covering them with sand. After 15 minutes or so the ritual was complete and they returned to the sea.

Looking farther down the beach revealed the tide had gone out and had exposed parts of a living reef. Sea grass covered these areas which were made up of a myriad of shells and had coalesced into a single slab of mostly calcium carbonate. The local bird population soon discovered that pools of water near these blocks held fish trapped by the tide. 'Easy pickin's' someone once said. Yet another component of the cycle of life where it propagates out of the sea.

Many years ago, Linus Pauling postulated that life could begin with a few simple ingredients. Essentially a lightning bolt, water, Hydrogen and volcanic fumes, when combined cause the creation of amino acids. Much later the life that was created in this primordial soup would millions of years hence crawl up on the rocks near the Ocean's edge and eventually onto land.

"The rocks were green then as well," thought Angela, "just like the ones below me at the seashore."

She imagined a time condensed parade of life from this very spot as she rested her head on the railing from the balcony. Her mind's eye witnessed the countless tides depositing life's organisms at the water's interface with the land. Nothing could stop the progression nor the evolution. She looked out at sea and could imagine the ancient sharks and Coelacanth swimming around the reefs just off shore. For millions of years the seashore within eyesight teemed with countless species, new ones were created and others became extinct every year. This continued until modern times, with the advent of intelligent species, notably human beings.

She observed the irony of these people walking by the ancient rocks today, cognizant that only humans could destroy the process. She also hoped that that would never happen; too much beauty. She also thought about how human beings were also the sole source of the methods to explore the future. Her work was endemic to this progress. Hours from now, an example of her creations would soar into the cosmos. Looking left she could just make out the launch gantry, which supported the rocket. Workers were just now starting to fuel the bird, carefully following a choreographed check list.

With binoculars or a long focal length camera lens, you could just make out the rocket body, with the umbilicals attached and surrounded by dancing vapors of liquid oxygen and hydrogen burning off at a set rate to keep the tanks perfectly filled. Each process and component had a history that went back decades. Decades that included catastrophic failures and heroic accomplishments. NASA and its associated aerospace companies had learned how to launch hardware into space with a high degree of success. It was expensive though, not just in terms of dollars but also in terms of lives and ruined equipment. Every single step of a rocket's production is choreographed, measured and evaluated. Every single screw, panel, wire, and transistor is screened, quality controlled, bagged, tagged, released, installed with great care and reevaluated to make sure every step was done properly.

The details are daunting but necessary. In fact if there is ever a failure, of any sort, a panel of experts are convened to discuss the event and recommend corrective actions. These were always serious matters. For now though, she thought about the enormous amount of work that went into her creation that was now sitting atop a tube full of highly explosive fuel. One of a million things could go wrong but probably wouldn't. She smiled at the thought and decided to relax and view the activities below her balcony.

At this time of year, the snow birds would show up, escaping the cold of the Northern U.S. and come down to warm up. Near Kennedy Space Center the temperatures seem to always be in the 70s and 80s; comfortable most of the time. The locals could be distinguished by their surfboards and their willingness to hit the waves early in the morning. Many of the younger ones surf before and after school and become

very accomplished at it as well. There are contests and every once in a while, professional photographers capturing the elegance of the art of surfing. There is something attractive about riding nature's motions. Just like flying or scuba diving and many other activities.

Riding the waves by the way happens in space as well. Currents of gravitational energy exist between large bodies like the Earth and Moon. Called manifolds, these interfaces exist at the neutral point of attraction and has been used successfully as a way to make significant course changes for spacecraft exploring our solar system. These substantial changes are made with minimal energy but of course timing is critical.

It turns out the Universe is filled with these manifolds and the reality is that we exist in a constantly undulating series of calculations, some simple some complex. But ultimately there is an explanation for everything. From this we gain the ability to predict the future. Angela knew this and understood that it would just be a matter of time for the computation capabilities of spacecraft electronics to be able to ride the gravity waves like surfers at the beach. She smiled at the prospect as she watched several proficient surfers glide over, and take every speck of energy out of the waves just off her balcony.

"Life is good," she thought. A seemingly random thought but rooted in her recent understanding of the flowing tributaries of energy that allow the planets to form and the stars to produce light to allow life to proliferate.

"And I am part of the process," she continued to think with a bit of pride.

"And I hope things go well this evening with the launch, its one of those small steps."

She poured herself an iced tea and settled back for the several hour wait until the launch. Glancing at her cell phone, she realized that it had been quiet for a long time, which was a good sign. A few more hours looking at the surf, the ocean in general and to the left, the launch complex, would do her heart well.

So..what's the deal with the young? She pondered their advantages and how they were in many ways fearless, or at least until they were a bit older. Fearless in an intellectual as well as a physical sense as their minds would go to great and mysterious places long before the older ones will. Additionally, the mathematically gifted many times performed their best work early in life. Alternatively, the philosophers tend to figure it out later in life.

That was part of the great mix, adding color to the canvas as well as defining a path through life. She sipped her iced tea and watched the beach. It was nice to be off work. Too many hours recently and as a result she was starting to feel numb. In her business, there were ebbs and flows as the engineering tasks changed in magnitude during a program. Her company was keen to give her more work during the slow periods which divided her attention from the main design efforts but kept her efficient. This was not a mundane life, programs changed, tasks varied and management went through modifications all the time. Also, it was not uncommon for engineers to change jobs frequently, with an average of 4 to 6 years at any one company. It depended on the skill set. Too specific of a talent and an engineer would find him or herself moving from state to state for the better paying jobs. In Angela's case, she worked at an antenna company as a designer, so there was steady work for a long period of time. She had settled in both at the company and in the community.

She lived on the beach and had the opportunities to view rocket launches, which occurred about once a month. About a year after she moved in, she had the great luck of seeing a Boeing 747-200 carry a retired space shuttle from the launch facilities at Cape Kennedy to Washington DC to be displayed in the Smithsonian. As a nod to the contributions of the space coast where she lived, the shuttle and 747 flew down the beach and over the town which housed many thousands

34

of space workers who had contributed so much to this flying dream. They said the shuttle was "the most complex machine ever built." Looking at it sitting on the launch pad did that notion a great disservice as it looked simple enough. Just a couple of solid rocket boosters strapped to a standard Hydrogen and Oxygen carrying tank bolted to a metal glider. The truth revealed its self to anyone who was lucky enough to get close to one of these devices. Like Michelangelo's Pieta at 20 meters, it looked cool enough, but up close it revealed the artistry and engineering genius too difficult to replicate again. As it turns out, her father had worked, as a secretarial assistant, on the shuttle.

Normally he was a professor of political science and economics but one summer, when money was scarce he took a job essentially typing the users manual for the shuttle flight computers. As he was also had been a jazz pianist for many years and could type over ninety words a minute, which made him a star in the cubical world of the aerospace company responsible for these computers. He discovered a group of highly intelligent individuals, both engineers and support staff, that matter-of-factly designed, built and tested a trio of orbiter computers that talked and arbitrated amongst themselves.

If one disagreed with the others, it was voted down and flagged for later examination. Any one of the three could navigate and control the spacecraft. Unlike the Apollo spacecraft which only had one computer, the shuttle's brain had company to confer with. One of a thousand bits of genius that comprised this vehicle. It hopped off of the pad significantly faster than the Apollo, shed its boosters minutes after launch, rode the external tank to low orbit, dropped it and entered the desired orbit to deploy satellites, observatories, laboratories and space station components. The back of the shuttle had an area some 59 feet long and fifteen feet wide that could carry 53,600 pounds into low Earth Orbit. It started with 4.4 million pounds of weight, mostly fuel and landed with 230,000 pounds (a 19:1 ratio) after gliding to a runway in either California or (more typically) Florida. Angela remembered the sonic booms upon its return, a double bang in the sky and marveled at their ability (due in part to the computers her father had helped to create) to land within hundreds of feet after millions of miles of flight.

Looking out to her right, she saw some lone fishermen in the line of sight of a Shuttle accident, where it had blown to bits and rained into the Atlantic Ocean. All in all, the Shuttle was 95% safe, but not yet ready for common passenger use.

Looking to her left, across the remaining balconies to the North, she spied a wall cloud, dark and menacing. It was in fact the precursor to a storm with, even in the mildest of forms, enormous amounts of energy, both electrical and pneumatic. Storms are just beginning to be understood, millions of measurements have been made of their innards, millions of simulations have been performed to watch their evolution, and millions of hours have been spent by scientists trying to understand their nature. But nature (no pun intended) is the key. The storms have a life cycle and are borne from unstable air, a lifting mechanism and moisture. Fronts, the movement of the Earth, the sun and moisture from

evaporation all contribute to the formation of storms. Their life cycle begins with the lifting of warm moist air from lower altitudes to higher altitudes. Then as the storm matures, the updrafts turn into updrafts and down drafts. This is the most violent time of the storm and has shredded many an aircraft that had the misfortune or arrogance to try to penetrate it. The typical outcome of flying into these storms, especially the monster, so called super cells, is the creation of aluminum confetti. This is why all commercial aircraft are required to have a radar, so they can navigate around the danger and live to fly another day. Pilots who have had the misfortune of testing the most benign areas of thunderstorm activity and lived describe violent updrafts shearing into violent downdrafts. The FAA recommends to pilots that if they are caught in one of these monsters, worry only about keeping the wings level, nothing else.

Wind shear and turbulence will play havoc with altitude and airspeed control, so its best to slow down and hold on. We notice this in simple, light turbulence, where the pilot slows down to make it through the area of bumps. Aircraft are amazingly strong and can take significantly more abuse that a human can, the problem with thunderstorms is that even aircraft are like tissue paper to the hammer of Mother Nature. But ironically, these violent beasts so prevalent in our Universe, are also beautiful. They create rainbows and extraordinary cloud formations. They also mimic the movement of the Milky Way and stellar clouds, as they spin in the form of hurricanes or tornados. The similarity is just a matter of scale.

Low pressure areas of weather rotate counter clockwise and high pressure areas rotate clockwise, in the Northern Hemisphere, opposite in the Southern. It's a matter of gravity and fluid dynamics which can be extrapolated to the galaxies and so many other planets like our own.

The energy Angela observed was humbling, the cruise ship on the horizon, sailing through the weather with ease, was a testament to the will of science and human endeavor. Problem solving is how we explore and travel to the stars. Engineers like her spend their time exercising their genetic powers to move civilization forward. In less than one hundred years, engineers went from flying a plane for the first time to flying a space station. Its was a just a matter of course to them but they moved humanity ahead by magnitudes. She smiled at the realization that she was helping this process move forward.

The evening was upon her, distant clouds were starting to grow into storms. Updrafts were to be followed by a maelstrom of updrafts and downdrafts. Their beauty however was undeniable from a distance. They seemed to be forming in a line, perhaps a front, as warm air overran cold or cold air overran warm. Instabilities and moisture grew these entities. They morphed quickly from simple cotton ball shapes to complex multi level juggernauts in front of her eyes. She sat back in her chair to enjoy the sunset and how it played with the cloud colors.

She thought, "I wonder if there is a relationship between the brewing storms and the terminator?" In other words, as the temperature lowered at sunset she wondered if that intensified or attenuated the energy. Hard to say, especially when so many tornadoes come at night. The scientific answer to this question is "it depends."

So too are so many answers to complex questions. "It depends" relates to weather, physics, astronomy and life. "It's interesting", she thought that the best questions in the Universe had a spectrum of answers, not with diametrically opposed answers she realized, just requiring a better understanding of the question.

Now at the end of the day, she could put everything in perspective. Her work, her life, her hopes and aspirations. They were all connected globally as well as locally, with her very busy day a metaphor for her life.

Now it was time for dinner, she moved to the kitchen and considered the options. "Mrs. Butterworth?" A random thought after witnessing an impressive sunset which reminded her of the image. Luckily the balcony wrapped around her building enough to allow her to see both sunrises and sunsets. "No, not Mrs. Butterworth for dinner, something more healthy." "Maybe pizza" she thought, certainly an option after a very busy day. She ordered a medium sausage and pineapple from the local Italian restaurant which of course was nondescript and therefore fantastic. During the wait, she puttered around the condo and cleaned what looked to be the worst of the offenders. The pizza arrived and again drawn to the balcony, she prepared a few slices, found a napkin and walked outside to enjoy the early evening.

The best descriptor for the view was 'pastel'. The sun moved West and drained its light with its journey. Nature is always aware of this, animals all respond to the change and prepare for alternate behavior during the night. Sounds attenuate, movement slows and a transition occurs to keep all creatures safe.

For her, she was aware of the change and appreciative of the pizza. Maybe more so the latter, as it (as expected) was wonderful.

The smells also changed with the light, as did the sounds. Quieter now and fresher, the sea breeze danced about the balcony while the sound of the waves harmonized. "This was a beautiful place," she thought. Harmony was indeed the key. She sat back, looked towards the water, then retrieved a glass of wine. Now to watch the sunset, which was unusually nice tonight. This was the terminator's march, the "Sunrise Descending" part of the day, where new things were being freshly illuminated at the exact opposite point of the globe. The impending darkness on this side however would now reveal the stars and galaxies. To many, this was the most important part of the "day."

The phone rang again, it was the Cape.

"The rocket is ready to go, all systems nominal, your equipment is working flawlessly."

"Thank you, I appreciate the update. I will be watching from the balcony."

"Wish I was there," said the voice of a hopeful suitor. "We can work on that," she replied with just a hint of optimism in her voice.

It was always a balance of words with this person. The interest was was definitely there, but the pace of the potential relationship had to be controlled to as not to over anticipate or set oneself up for disappointment. She thought about him for a few moments more and considered her real dreams about the future, but the wine was starting to morph her thinking.

"I shouldn't think about this any more, and maybe slow down on the alcohol. Might have to go back to the Cape if there is a problem," she thought. "Although once the bird is lit, they won't need my help for days."

Smiling at this reasoning and perhaps flattered by the male attention, she took another sip, almost with abandon. "Just a few more hours to go."

The stars were starting to come out along with the possibility of some storms. The clouds, at the light's last gasp looked more like cumulous than stratus, this would delay the launch. The Cape had very strict rules regarding launch criteria. Lightning could not get within 20 miles of the pad and the upper level winds, which were being monitored by special radars, could not show signs of shearing or instability. These radar, called "Profilers" looked straight up and could sense the velocity and direction of the air in layers all the way up to 50,000 feet. The normal

conditions showed winds going the same way for the most part from near the surface (actually slightly above the boundary layer) to the stratosphere. Sometimes upper air disturbances, certainly ones that spawn thunderstorms can cause significant shear or winds going opposite directions, which are dangerous for rockets as well as aircraft.

She rose to check her computer and see if there would be a delay. She found none but noticed that the radar returns this evening were starting to reveal some increased activity.

"Rats, I hope it still goes," she thought. "But for now, what a display."

The darkness was getting deeper which allowed the contrast of the developing storms to be more stark. Clouds lit up as if they had a million strobe lights within them and periodically, a bolt would emanate from beneath a cloud and propagate to the water. The amount of energy on display was awe inspiring, especially if these bolts came closer.

They were starting to proliferate now, and even thunder could be heard above the crashing waves. She sobered a bit. Going back to the computer though showed her that the storms were actually part of a line of weather that would move quickly past her and the launch pad. This brought some relief.

"Okay, then just relax," she thought, "conditions will improve and they know what they are doing at launch control."

Indeed they did, as dozens of engineers and technicians were watching every detail, especially the weather. The launch director periodically polled the lead system's engineers for their opinions to "come out of hold." Most if not all of these people reported "Go" with the exception of the person in charge of weather. His opinion so far was "No go." Everyone knew however that this was a passing line of activity and behind it was clear, smooth air.

Most if not all of these engineers were experienced and knew that if the weather person was not looking exasperated, there was a good chance of a launch.

They continued to monitor and periodically glance over to the weather desk to see what his mood was revealing.

Knowing this, Angela could envision the scene and the glances. "Professionals being professional," she thought with a wry smile.

Back to the light show however showed more interesting activity. Storms were starting to collide and fuse, increasing the activity. She could actually see the movement of the upper portions of the clouds, such violent action was due to enormous wind shear activity, where column of unstable air were rising in close proximity to columns that were descending. The velocities were in the hundreds of miles per hour. This would turn a rocket into confetti if there were unlucky enough to try to try and penetrate it.

The launch of course was on hold by now. The upper winds had increased and had become unstable. This situation was beyond the capabilities of even the best rocket autopilots. In addition, the optical recording equipment could not keep track of the vehicle due to the low cloud deck.

"Amazing," she thought. "What enormous energy is in those clouds."

Although the forecast was for a line of thunderstorms to pass quickly, the ferociousness of the event was obvious. By now the launch personnel were inside, the rocket was secure with its "strong back" and the four towers surrounding the launch pad were absorbing and dissipating the static charges that were now surrounding it.

Clusters of storms continued to coalesce and increase in strength. The main band was now overhead, with clouds exceeding 50,000 feet in height. Interestingly, some of the purest air to breath was now descending on Angela and the balcony as the downdrafts were pulling air from very high altitudes downward and splashing it upon the ground.

53

It reminded her of taking flying lessons a few years ago, when she realized that the vast majority of people on this Earth live in thick, dusty air. It became obvious when they would take off in their Cessna on a calm day and within a thousand feet or less, pass from the haze to the clear cool air. It really was easier to breath.   Now on her balcony, she recognized the smell and taste of it.

She also remembered flying one evening in glass smooth air, with a full moon above over newly fallen snow. The sensation was very overwhelming in that it really felt like the Earth was moving but she was not. At that time she really felt like she could just open the door and walk

54

outside. This even as she was moving at over 100 miles an hour.

"Ah, the joys of flying."

So she waited for the storms to abate and thought about the rocket flying through the smooth air after the wind died down, much like she in her Cessna, it would feel a few bumps close to the ground, then smoother and smoother air would follow.   This until there was no air at all and the Earth really would be spinning below.

She was jealous at the thought. It was however getting more and more frequent for robots and people to go into space, this launch was no exception. Somehow human beings had learned to harness energy chemically and electromagnetically to get themselves to the moon and beyond.   This started of course from the ancient wonderment of watching nature, like she was now.

A few more straggler storms were now passing through, the tail end of the line of thunderstorms. She adjusted in her seat then rose to get a glass of water.

The laptop that had been running besides her showed the activity in the launch control room. It had been quiet as the controllers waited for the storm to pass. Now however, they were starting to move around periodically glance at the controller who was in charge of weather observations. His mood would predict theirs.

At this time he was checking control panels and watching e-mail traffic amongst the weather staff in several other local facilities. They were now measuring calmer conditions and to the West, clearing skies.

After a few last spectacular lightning bolts, the energy of the event started to dissipate. Angela was now experiencing calm winds, a quiet ocean and cooler temperatures.

At the launch control room, the weather controller was smiling and at one point looked over to the director and smiled. This was the clue that they could now start the process of getting the rocket ready for launch. All of the controllers now heard the official report.

"Launch director, Met here, we are releasing the weather hold."

The response...

"Okay, listen up everyone, reset the count to T minus 57 minutes. Retract the strong back and start the launch sequence on my mark......Mark!"

Now there was real action in the room Angela could tell from her laptop. The launch could really happen, this made her smile. She would wait for the first glass of wine for the evening until it was obvious she was

no longer needed. The satellite which was continuously monitored would go on internal power about 15 minutes before launch. This would freeze any actions on the systems she was responsible for. In 24 hours they would be operational as the satellite would by that time be safely in a parking orbit.

They would not need her until then, which would give her a long break.

Now however people were descending on the beach as they usually did at night, maybe a few more because of the launch. They brought flashlights to look for crabs and treasure. No one wants to step on a crab and there were hundreds moving around in the dark. Angela set up her camera and took time lapse pictures of the lights as the people moved around. She set the exposure time to 30 seconds per frame and took several shots. They looked ghostly and surreal.

She watched as groups of people as well as individuals moved around looking at various places on the beach. For Angela, this was almost a nightly occurrence. It would appear however to a non native as a strange sight.

"T minus 45 minutes."

She paused to reflect on the moment and watch the post sunset beachcombers. People came to this beach any time of year and if they came from any reasonable distance, they intended to have fun. Many times Angela watched people out in poor weather or at strange hours. If they had spent substantial money to get here then nothing was going to stop their vacation plans, not even weather.

She watched them for a while longer then went back to her laptop where the details of the rocket launch were being displayed. The beachcombers continued to explore beneath her while she wondered how many of them knew what was about to transpire. Millions of pounds of thrust were about to be unleashed just a few miles away. Like several launches before, many beachcombers were shocked to see the light (especially at night) and later hear the low roar of the engines.

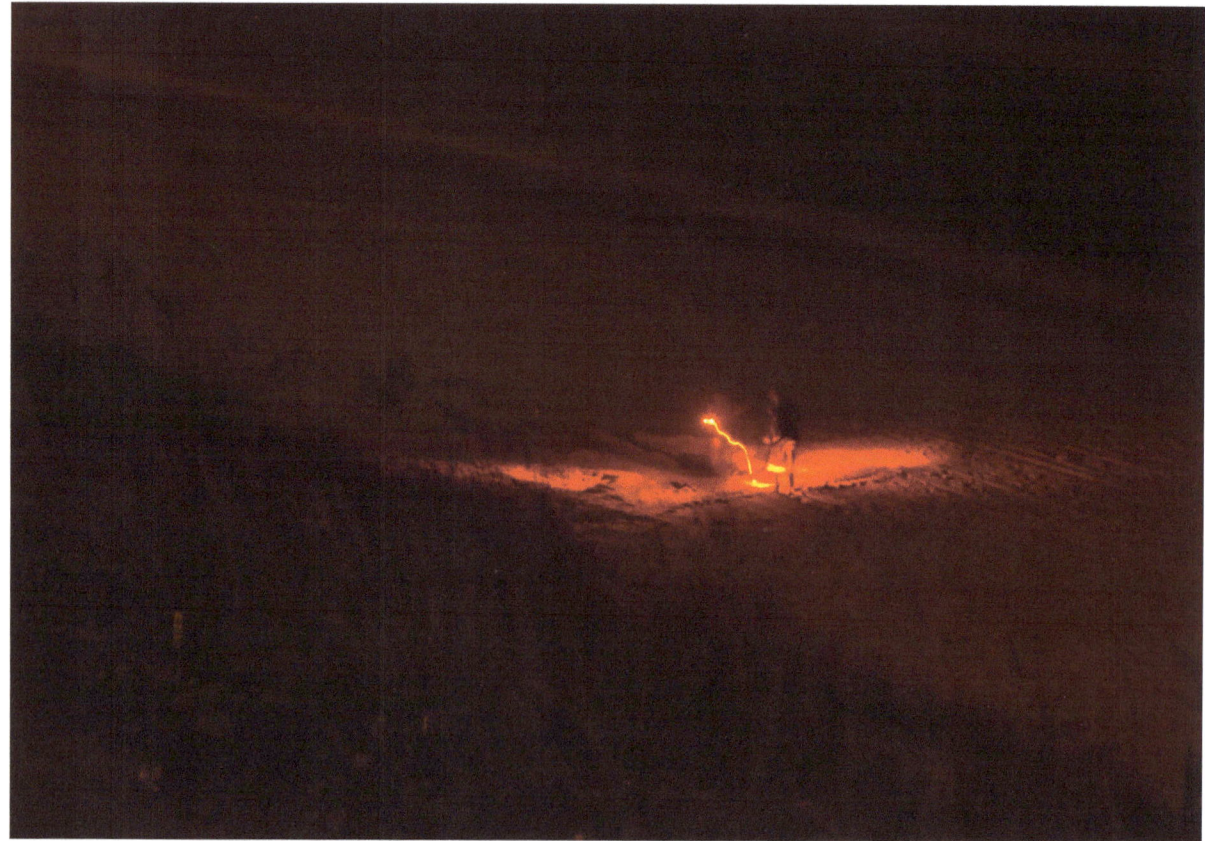

The speed of flight is also an amazing sight, where within approximately one minute the rockets go from standing to near 700 miles an hour. Within about eight minutes, they are in space. Several night launches can be visibly followed to almost Africa if the orbital insertion angle is optimum. Way cool to witness.

Once, she took a camera and a tripod out to a local beach that was very dark at the time in anticipation of a rocket launch. This beach was just a few miles from the launch pad and quiet except for the roar of the ocean. Carefully she found her way to a small sand hill and set up her equipment. After several test exposures, she felt that she had the right settings and then started to watch her smart phone for updates on the launch. At one minute before launch, she prepared to start a long exposure that would capture the initial launch sequence through the first

minute of flight, where the rocket would be at or beyond the speed of sound.   In the last few seconds, she held her breath and placed her finger just above the shutter button. Then there was an unexpected blinding light from the engine firings and a very quick rumble and roar that was also unexpectedly loud. She realized quickly that she was much closer than she had thought and that the exposures she set up would be completely washed out.

Also, with the now daylight conditions, she also discovered that she was surrounded by people who had separately wandered out onto the beach probably unaware of the others in close proximity. The effect was surreal and as the rocket rose in altitude, the darkness once again descended on the landscape and the inhabitants disappeared into the encroaching gray.

"T minus 30 minutes."

She had to recover a bit from the shock of the launch, but managed to find her way back to the car and later, examine the mostly washed out photos she had taken. Now however, she watched the beachcombers and their light displays.

In the distance the rocket was illuminated against the evening sky.

Time for a glass of wine as the chances of her getting a call after T minus thirty minutes was extremely slim. By now the satellite had been active and passing self tests for a very long time. Soon, it would go on internal power. This meant that the batteries would supply all energy to the satellite bus. There could be communications of course but when a satellite reaches this state, it is ready for launch.

Also, at this time the rocket itself was securing itself by confirming it has a navigation lock and that all of the tanks, which have been filled for some time now, have the right temperature, pressure and fill levels.

The ground computers were also doing a significantly less amount of work. Soon the guidance and all other computer functions will be under internal power and autonomy. Much like removing training wheels or letting your child walk to school for the first time, the rocket, more correctly referred to as an autonomous entity, was making its own decisions and letting all who were concerned that everything was working properly.

"T minus 20 minutes."

Now the tanks on all stages were completely filled with their respective propellants and the plumes of excess fuel sprayed from the sides of the rocket. This condition would last until the rocket actually departed the pad.

Angela knew the sequence that would be followed as she sat back and sipped her wine, smiling of course. Looking to the South she could see the beginnings of the final activities on the launch pad. The spot lights would soon be illuminating.

"What an amazing experience to have, she thought." A rocket launch with her handiwork soon, wine in hand, perfect weather, beachcombers wandering about and a full moon later tonight.   It doesn't get much better. With that in mind, she rose to get a second glass of wine.

"T minus 10 minutes"

Guidance was now on "internal," tanks were completely pressurized, the range safety officers were doing their final checks and they would experience a "hold" at T minus 8 minutes. This would allow the launch director to perform the final canvas of the flight controllers, of which there were 12. The final one would be weather. Tonight it was looking good as the storms have moved completely out.

A new glass in hand, Angela made her way back to the balcony for the final series of events.

"T minus 8 minutes"

The anticipated hold had started, the launch director was now polling the specialist directors.....

"CBC?"
"Go"
"Range?"
"We're go"
"TMR?
"Go"
"Safety?"
"Go"
"SMS?"
"Go!"
"Weather?"
"We're go."

"This is the launch director, resume countdown."

"T minus 8 minutes and counting."

"All systems on internal."

"All tanks pressures nominal."

"T minus 60 seconds and counting"

"T minus 30 seconds"

"T minus 20 seconds"

"T minus 10 seconds"

"9...8...7...6...5...4...3...engine ignition 2...1..liftoff, we have liftoff, liftoff of the Dragon 9 booster with the Dawn II satellite system, for the exploration of the solar system and beyond."

"T plus 10 seconds, speed 200 miles per hour, altitude 10,000 feet. "

"T plus 20 seconds, speed 500 miles an hour, altitude 30,000 feet, the rocket is now 50 miles down range"

"The rocket is now going the speed of maximum Q, throttling back to minimize excessive vibration. Speed 700 miles per hour, altitude 50,000 feet."

"Engines now at full thrust, speed 900 miles per hour. 100 miles down range. All systems nominal. Vectors within safe bands."

"Altitude 80,000 feet, coming up on main engine cutoff."

"Main engine throttled back, separation in 5 seconds."

"We have a successful separation, second stage ignition in 5 seconds."

"Second stage at full thrust, flight path nominal, tank pressures, pump pressures and temperatures nominal."

"Altitude 150,000 feet, speed 2,000 miles per hour, 400 miles down range."

"Altitude 200,000 feet, speed 3,000 miles per hour, 700 miles down range."

"All systems nominal, 1200 miles down range, 300,000 feet altitude. Nose cone sep in 5 seconds."

"We have a successful separation, attitude nominal, spacecraft nominal."

"Altitude 400,000 feet, speed 7,000 miles per hour."

"We have a successful launch of the Valkyrie satellite, bringing a new understanding of the makeup of our solar system."

Angela sat back in wonderment. She had seen many launches before but her fingerprints were on this one. She felt a mixture of happiness, proudness, worthiness and contentment at the launch. The voice overs of the launch had now ceased but she could still see the progress of the rocket through the heavens. It was awe inspiring, all of her hard work, over the many years and this display confirmed that the effort was worth while.

She smiled for a long time, oblivious to who might see her grinning like a cheshire cat on her balcony, wondering what the big deal might be. She looked and felt wonderful.

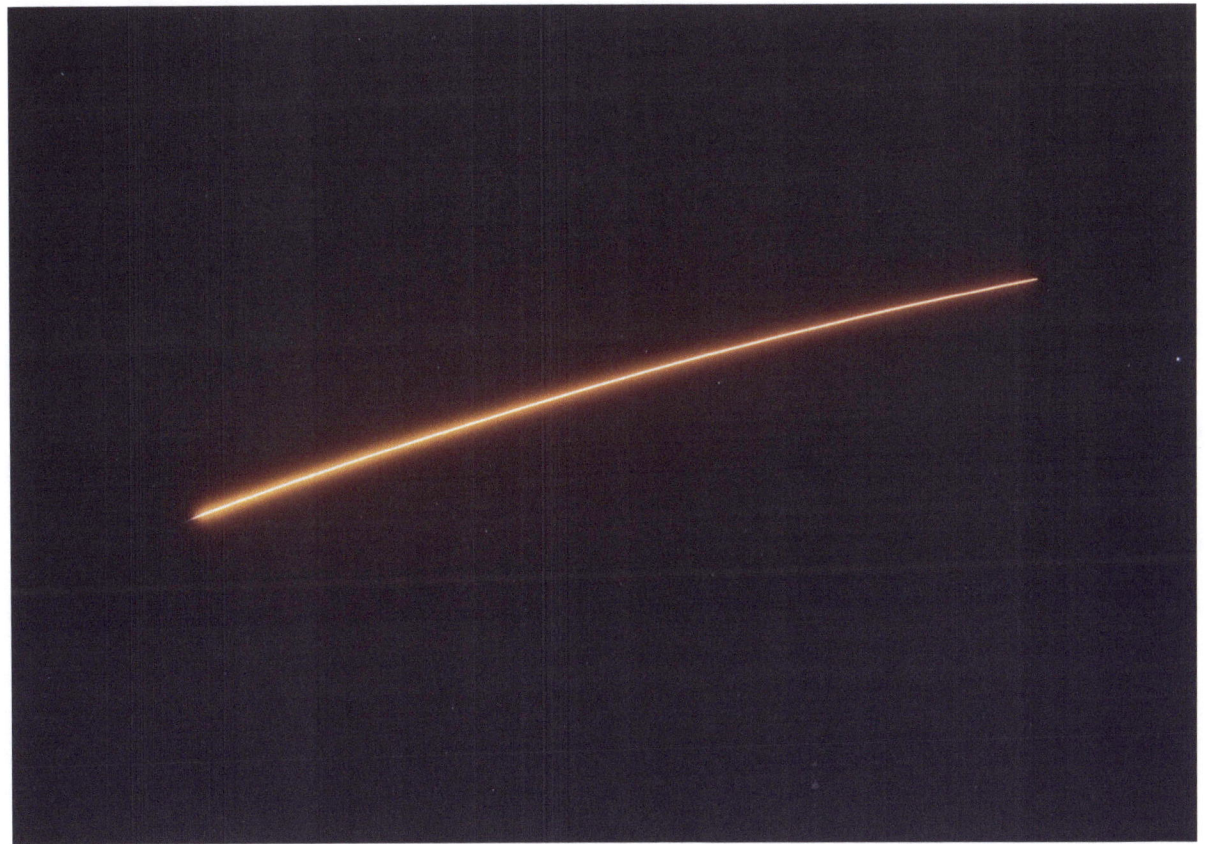

The rocket arced over the ocean right in front of the balcony. The stars were out and provided a nice backdrop to the machine headed in their direction. The color of the plume was from a mixture of liquid oxygen and kerosine. This and liquid hydrogen were the preferred mixtures. Interesting that the most potent rocket fuel is water. The shuttle, Apollo and many other rockets used this combination. The "exhaust pollution" was water vapor as the two gases recombined in a very energy efficient explosive way. So water creates life and allows us to voyage to the stars. There are vast quantities of the compound in space, in interstellar clouds, comets, planets and moons. She wondered if the future space missions would hop between oases and gather more fuel for the next leg of their journey.

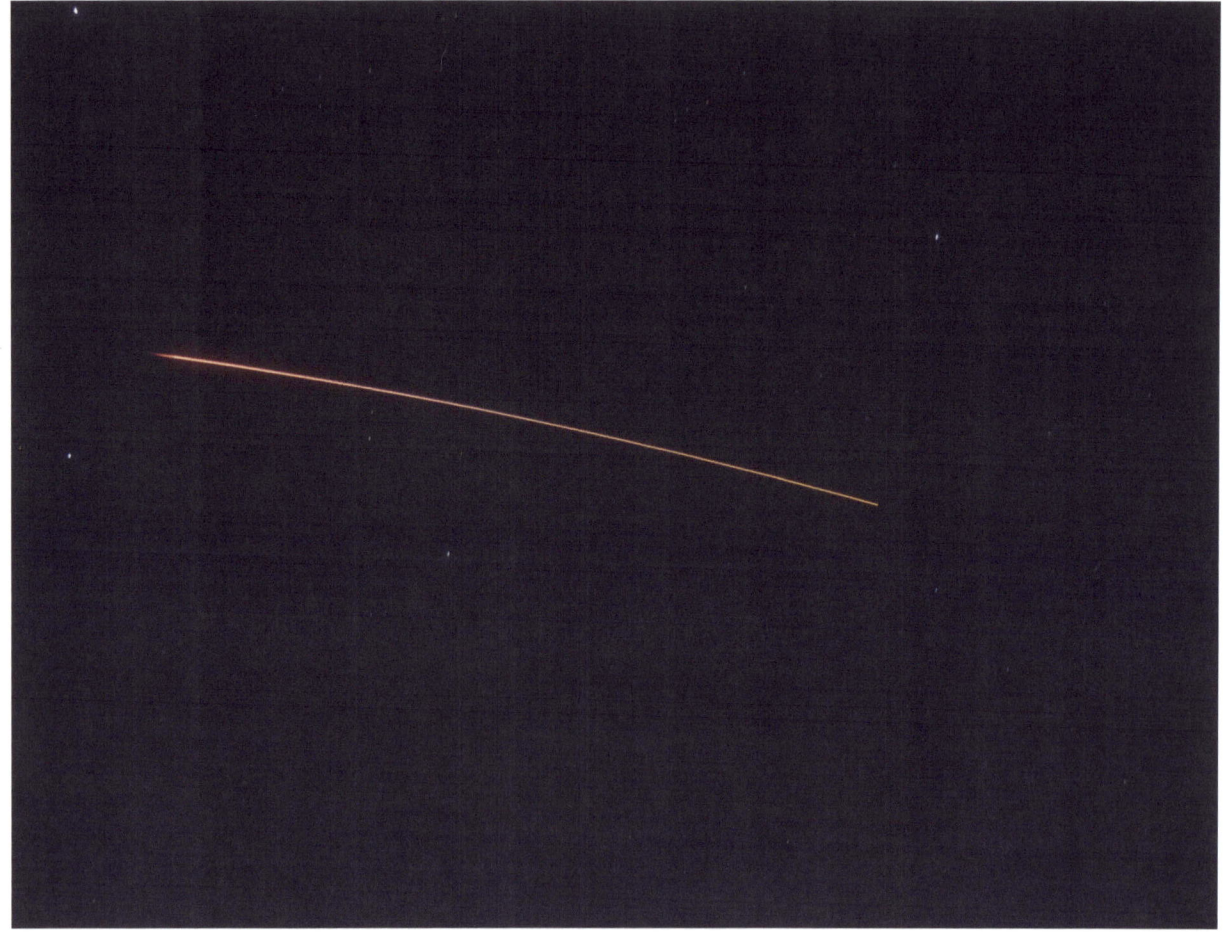

Also, there is another interesting fact about water, it is one of the very best ways to protect humans from space radiation. Just like atomic physicists had discovered many decades ago, placing a nuclear

reactor in a pool of water was a very safe thing to do. NASA had also considered placing astronauts in a protective cocoon of water then they travel to Mars and beyond.

So maybe Thales was right so many thousands of years ago when he postulated that all things come from water. Life evolved from it, we need it to sustain our bodies, it allows us to leave Earth and the Universe is filled with it.

She looked again at the rocket, now starting to get faint as it was entering orbit. It was streaking across the constellation Orion now and about to "stage." This is where the last portion of the rocket takes the payload to its intended orbit. There would be a brief time where the rocket drifted in space while it shed its second stage, then the third and final stage would ignite and place the payload in a highly elliptical orbit. The high point would be near the final orbital position. Thrusters would make the final adjustments.

She could now see the staging and the final faint glimpses of the payload with her handiwork in it.

"What a beautiful launch," she thought. "We are going to the stars someday and this is how it will start. And not soon enough if it was up to me."

Sitting back in her chair she listened to what was left from the launch followed by a peaceful lapping of the ocean on the beach.

"My systems are starting to wake up now and tomorrow we will know how everything went. We tested this so much I can't see how anything could go wrong. And what it will be doing, helping mankind come closer, communicate better and promote science and understanding."

Next up this evening was the moonrise. A full moon in fact which rose predictably and is the basis for so many calendars. It rose full, just to cap off a perfect evening. It appeared to rise into the clouds, then out again, causing the ocean to sparkle and scintillate like a million diamonds.

Water had recently been found on the moon. This was mostly unexpected but emphasized the point that this fluid is everywhere. Other recent discoveries of the many thousands of planets around the thousands of stars in a small portion of the visible universe also spoke to the fact that life out there was prolific.

They had found life on Earth in some of the most challenging environments; thousands of feet below the surface in the deepest oceans, in the clouds, in the frozen wastelands of the poles. It was actually hard not to find it.

It turns out that exo-planets in the "Goldilocks" zone, where the temperature were much like that on Earth, had been found roughly the size of our own planet and in the vicinity of water. The radio telescope in Northern Chile, ALMA, had made the most detailed maps of the regions around stars and their planets.

These maps showed the ratios of elements and compounds near or on these planets much like our own. What became obvious was that life was everywhere, easy to start, hard to extinguish.

Recent searches of interstellar molecules had found thousands of individual types from the most simple, like Hydrogen, to the very complex carbon compounds.

Water of course is everywhere, including emanating from comets, moons and masering from vast clouds in interstellar space. Oxygen, Carbon Dioxide, Formaldehyde and Carbon Monoxide are in vast amounts as well.

Now the moon was rising majestically above the clouds and ocean, she zoomed her camera in for a close up shot and could now see the maria, or seas of our moon. The crater Tyco was also clear. From the area to her left the Apollo moon rockets lifted off and sent people to the Sea of Tranquility as well as several other places. They left instruments, rovers, and foot prints. Lately however the ingenuity of students, engineers and scientist have created lunar robots and have sent them to the moon inexpensively. The young people today do not see this as a

massive national challenge, they see it as homework and fun. This attitude will get us to those planets we can now detect and start the process of discovery and colonization. "What a great time to be alive," she thought. "This is when humans figured out how to get to space, or maybe more accurately, how to respond to our need to explore those other worlds around the stars we have watched and created mythology for over the last many thousands of years."

A cruise ship was now passing from the Port of Cape Canaveral out to the Bahamas. On board were thousands of vacationers, who had just

observed a rocket launch from the deck of their ship. They must have been impressed by the sight, especially considering how close they must have been this evening.

She adjusted the camera to take a 10 second exposure, leaving light streaks of many colors. This reminded her of some of Einstein's theories, for instance when a spaceship moves closer to the speed of light, it will elongate just like the image she was witnessing.

"Einstein is still talking," she thought. "His mind took us to places no one could have imagined at the time of his writings. He is still taking us to new places. He corrected the flawed thinking of his era and gently pointed us towards new, more achievable goals. Now we are discovering so much more than we could have without him."

This fact allows the engineers like Angela Bencomo to make the calculations, design the hardware and point our future to the stars.

Some notable quotes that influenced this book:

Konrad Lorenz, "Space exploration safely absorbs man's aggressive and competitive instincts, and in applauding the astronauts' exploits, we are grasping at a hope of preserving peace on earth." Anne Morrow (wife of Charles Lindberg) quoting in her book 'Earth Shine'

"Without adventure, civilization is in full decay." Albert North Whitehead

"There is only one perfect road and that road is ahead of you, always ahead of you." Sri Chinmoy

"So often time it happens, we all live our life in chains, and we never even know we have the key". The Eagles, "Already Gone"

"I'm coming back in… and it's the saddest moment of my life."

Ed White expresses his sorrow at the conclusion of the first American spacewalk during the Gemini 4 mission on 3 June 1965.

ABOUT THE AUTHOR

Kevin Shoemaker was born in New York City in April of 1954. A son of an actress and musician turned professor. He has lived in several states and has been educated in the fields of philosophy, radio astronomy and antenna design. He has authored several technical papers in astronomy and has many patents in the fields of aviation, antenna design and meteorology. In addition, he is an avid pilot and boat owner and holds several certificates for operating airplanes, helicopters and performing flight instruction. Currently he works as an antenna and radar designer near Cape Canaveral. Mr. Shoemaker is a father of one daughter and one son and lives in Indian Harbour Beach.

Comments?   e-mail: Shoemakerlabs@gmail.com

Other books by the author:

Mars Life
Practical Antenna Design
The Voyages of Gaea
Sunrise Descending
Life in the Universe and Where to Find It